Warm as Wool

by Scott Russell Sanders

illustrated by Helen Cogancherry

Bradbury Press   New York

Maxwell Macmillan Canada   Toronto
Maxwell Macmillan International
New York   Oxford   Singapore   Sydney

Bradbury Press
Macmillan Publishing Company
866 Third Avenue
New York, NY 10022

Maxwell Macmillan Canada, Inc.
1200 Eglinton Avenue East
Suite 200
Don Mills, Ontario M3C 3N1

Macmillan Publishing Company is part of the Maxwell Communication
Group of Companies.

First American edition
Printed and bound in Hong Kong by South China Printing Company (1988) Ltd.
10 9 8 7 6 5 4 3 2 1
The illustrations were done in watercolor, with pencil highlights.
The text of this book is set in Berkeley Old Style Medium.
Typography by Julie Quan

LIBRARY OF CONGRESS CATALOGING-IN-PUBLICATION DATA
Sanders, Scott R. (Scott Russell), date.
Warm as wool / by Scott Russell Sanders / illustrated by Helen
Cogancherry. — 1st ed.
p.   cm.
Summary: When Betsy Ward's family moves to Ohio from Connecticut
in 1803, she brings along a sockful of coins to buy sheep so that
she can gather wool, spin cloth, and make clothes to keep her
children warm.
ISBN 0-02-778139-9
[1. Frontier and pioneer life—Fiction. 2. Ohio—Fiction.
3. Sheep—Fiction.] I. Cogancherry, Helen, ill. II. Title.
PZ7.S19786War 1992
[Fic]—dc20   91-34987

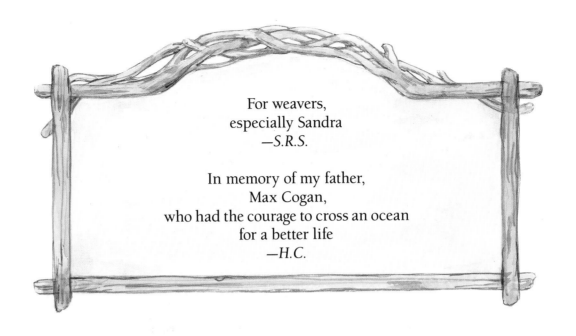

For weavers,
especially Sandra
—*S.R.S.*

In memory of my father,
Max Cogan,
who had the courage to cross an ocean
for a better life
—*H.C.*

A Note from the Artist

Many thanks to Kristina Haughland at the Philadelphia Museum of Art costume department, to the staffs of the Swarthmore, Helen Kate Furness, and Ridley Township libraries, as well as to the Free Library of Philadelphia, Print & Picture Department. Thanks to the volunteers at the Colonial Plantation in Ridley Creek Park. Special thanks to Barbara Lalicki, my editor, who is a joy to work with.

PROLOGUE

BETSY WARD'S three children were cold. Their teeth started clicking soon after they left their old home in Connecticut, in September of 1803. They rode a rackety wagon through New York. They crossed Lake Erie in a tippy boat, rain in their faces, waves bucking under them like wild horses. They landed on the shore near Cleveland and squished through mud, past the village of Ravenna into the dark Ohio woods, where they made their new home.

All of December, the family slept in a lean-to, while Betsy Ward and her husband, Josiah, built a cabin out of logs from tulip poplar trees. The

roof was covered with bark. The door was a deerskin weighted down with a stick. The children daubed clay from the creek between the logs. And so they passed their first year in the wilderness.

Who were the children? Joshua was the oldest, a boy of eight, tall enough to see through the greased paper window, strong enough to carry two pails of water from the spring. Sarah was five, with a long pigtail and a short laugh, a wonder at throwing snowballs and climbing trees. Three-year-old William was quick as a fox at running and good at finding little things lost underfoot. Wherever Joshua and Sarah went, William scooted along beside them, talking a blue streak, poking his nose into everything from morning until night.

IT WAS AN ICY PLACE TO LIVE IN WINTER, THIS ROUGH CABIN in a clearing. No matter how much clay William and Sarah patted between the logs, no matter how many leaves Joshua raked against the walls outside, wind kept slicing through the gaps. Frost gathered on the dirt floor. Snow lit the woods with cold white light as far as the children could see, and drifts kept rising at the door.

The clothes the children had worn since moving out here to the Ohio frontier were tattered and frayed. Betsy Ward sewed patches on their patches, and still the cold played music on the children's ribs, the wind whistled about their knees.

Josiah Ward said, "Throw another bearskin on the bed. Wrap their feet in sacks when they go out to play."

But every bearskin in the cabin was already piled on the bed. The children already wore every stitch and rag they owned. And still they shivered and their teeth chattered.

Betsy Ward needed wool, lots of it, to make them cozy new clothes. From Connecticut she had brought a spinning wheel to spin wool into thread, a loom to weave it into cloth, and a sockful of coins to buy sheep. She had saved these coins for sheep, and she would spend them on nothing else. But what good were money and wheel and loom when there wasn't so much as a solitary lamb within a hundred miles of her farm?

And so when a herd of sheep drifted by the cabin one day in the spring, Betsy Ward imagined each animal a walking blanket, a four-legged frock, a pair of pantaloons on the hoof.

Joshua, Sarah, and William peeked out from behind her skirts at these strange animals. The sheep had walked from Pennsylvania, and their fleece was bedraggled with twigs and cockleburs and dirt. Josiah Ward thought they were pretty sorry-looking beasts. Betsy Ward did not give a hoot how filthy they were. Wool was wool, and would keep a body warm.

"How much do you want for those sheep?" she asked the drover.

Glancing at the log cabin, the man answered, "More than you've got."

"You're right about that," said Josiah Ward.

"Hold on there," said Betsy Ward. She hurried indoors, then returned, blinking, into the daylight. "I have a stocking here," she said, holding up the sockful of coins.

Josiah Ward and the children grinned, for they had forgotten about the sock. The drover stopped his herd. He stroked his chin. "I promised these sheep to Mr. Culver," he told her.

"Culver!" she scoffed. "He'll only let them eat poisonweed and kill themselves like he did the last ones." Betsy Ward took from the stocking a handful of coins.

"I see your point," said the drover. "Maybe I can spare you eight sheep."

The deal was swiftly made, and Betsy Ward owned eight of the ragamuffin beasts. Josiah Ward built a pen to hold them. The children petted the sheep, hugged them round the fat, fuzzy necks, even tried to ride them.

That night, while the sheep mulled about in the pen, Betsy
Ward sheared them all in her dreams. Come morning, she found
that two of them had been slaughtered by wolves.

She gathered the wool from the bodies, washed and carded
and spun it. She would weave it into cloth for breeches.

Every night afterward, she and her husband
locked the surviving sheep in the cabin. The
children, as they fell asleep, could hear the
animals breathing and could smell the
luscious oily hair.

Even if they'd had a hundred eyes, the Wards could not watch the sheep every minute. On a Sunday while the family sang hymns at the meetinghouse in Ravenna, one of the sheep ate poisonweed, swelled up, and died. Another sheep drowned in the creek on a day when the family was helping neighbors harvest corn. And another sheep, trotting alongside the children as they rolled barrel hoops, broke its leg in a groundhog hole. Betsy Ward set her mouth hard every time a sheep died, and she salvaged every last bit of fleece.

Of the three sheep still alive the following spring, only one was a ewe. But the ewe gave birth to lambs, which in due time gave birth to their own lambs, which grew woolly and fat on the lush grass, and so on, season after season, until Betsy Ward eventually owned an entire flock, all sprung from that stockingful of Connecticut coins.

Her wheel spun through the day,
her loom clacked into the night.

Dressed from head to toe in wool,
her children at last were warm.

BETSY AND JOSIAH WARD made their clearing and built their cabin in 1803, the year Ohio became a state. The nearest village was Ravenna, which became the seat of Portage County. When I grew up in that county a century and a half later, the landscape was still a handsome patchwork of woods and farms. Today, though many of the farms have failed, and commerce has crept along the highways, much of the land would still be familiar to those early homesteaders.

The village of Aurora, whose founding I described in my previous picture book, *Aurora Means Dawn,* is also in Portage County. Readers of the earlier book will know that I have long been trying to imagine the experiences of families who moved from the settled districts of the East, over the mountains, into the wild heart of the continent.

My tale about the Ward family began when I read, in a *History of Portage County* (1885), that "Mrs. Josiah Ward is credited with owning the first sheep in Randolph Township, which were brought in from the East in 1805. Her husband, having no money, was unable to purchase them, when she 'took out her stocking' and paid cash down for eight or ten of the drove standing in front of her little cabin. She had saved up this money ere leaving her Connecticut home, to be used for that very purpose." I pondered that sockful of coins, that woman's determination. When I read, later in the same history, that on their journey to Ohio "they came in an open boat up the lake, and suffered greatly from cold and many privations," I knew this was a story about the struggle to stay warm.

Suffering is part of the truth about the frontier. The settlers suffered, the native people suffered, the woods and soils and wild beasts suffered. Children can understand this, I believe, if we are honest with them. Children enter the past, as we all do, not through names and dates but through the feelings and thoughts of those who lived in that past.

Every story bears the imprint of the storyteller. My earliest memories are of clumping over furrows in a plowed field and rolling the words of songs on my tongue. Every child I know loves the sound and weight and taste of words. So I give them *rackety* and *squished*, *ragamuffin* and *pantaloons*. I know looms and the smell of raw wool, because my sister Sandra is a weaver. As I write these words, I am wearing a sweater knitted a dozen years ago by my wife. The oil still comes off on my fingers with the husky aroma of lanolin.

I hope that children will shiver when they hear this story, or when they read it to themselves. I hope they will rub their faces against wool sweaters, hug some patient grown-up about the knees, look for tiny lost things in the grass. And as they read or listen, I hope these children will climb into the arms of someone who loves them, and grow warm.

Scott Russell Sanders